Beautifully Crushed

Candied Crush #20

Charity Parkerson

Punk & SIssy Publications

Contents

Introduction   I

Chapter One   3

Chapter Two   21

Chapter Three   40

Chapter Four   51

Chapter Five   65

Chapter Six   81

Chapter Seven   94

Chapter Eight   121

About the Author   133

Introduction

❤

ALL KYE WANTS IS a nice guy. Sonny is that guy. Kye thinks he's full of it.

For months, Kye flirted his cute booty off to get Sonny to ask him out. After Sonny unexpectedly kissed him, Kye thought he was finally going to get his man. That was six weeks ago, and everything has changed. Now Kye can't stop hiding from Sonny and avoiding his calls. After Sonny stood him up, he's lost his chance as far as Kye is concerned. Kye has no interest in giving Sonny a second chance. End of story.

Kye makes Sonny insane. Sonny is as unused to being flirted with as he is to being the bad guy. Guys like Kye don't date guys like him. When he made dinner plans with Kye, Sonny can't explain what happened. He freaked. Now he's had time to think, and he realizes he's an idiot. Kye obviously genuinely liked him. Unfortunately, no matter how hard Sonny tries, Kye won't give him the time of day. Sonny has no clue how to fix it.

Kye and Sonny are looking for exactly what they could find in each other. If only they would stop overthinking everything and ruining their lives.

Chapter One

♥

FOR SIX SOLID WEEKS, Kye had been hiding each day when the delivery truck came. It was dumb. He was a child. Whatever. Kye knew all these things and couldn't help it. His feelings were hurt. It was that simple, and that complicated. Six weeks ago, he had been waiting at the door for Sonny, their delivery guy, to show up every single day. He had been like a dog waiting for its owner to get home. Then Sonny had kissed him, and they had set a time for a date. Kye had been over the moon with excitement. He had genuinely believed he was about to get his man. Then Sonny had stood him up.

Kye would freely admit he could be a bitch when crossed. His initial gut reaction had been to wait for Sonny's next delivery and show him what he had missed. The thing was, Kye wasn't so sure Sonny missed any damn thing. Kye had been so busy working nonstop for years, he hadn't dated in forever. He had put himself out there for Sonny. His chest hurt every time he thought about facing Sonny. That was why Kye hid in his office now, waiting for Aric to deal with him.

"Is Kye around?"

"Yes."

Kye wanted to cheer at the coldness in Aric's voice. When Kye's boss, Seth, had married Aric's boss, Baker, it had been a great day for Kye. Aric had become a good friend and the first line of defense against Sonny. Kye didn't know what he would do without him.

"Is it okay if I talk to him?"

"No."

At Aric's curt answer, Kye covered his mouth and pressed his ear harder against the door.

"Please?"

Aric released a loud sigh at Sonny's pleading tone. "He's not here."

"But you just said…"

Kye swore he could hear Aric staring at Sonny with zero remorse.

Sonny quickly reversed course. "Okay, then."

When Kye heard the chime on the door, letting him know Sonny had left, the sadness hit. A small part of him wanted to chase after Sonny. He had spent months wearing Sonny down before finally securing that date Sonny had missed. Kye felt dumb as hell. He had honestly thought Sonny was a nice guy. Kye had genuinely believed Sonny liked him. Now here he was, still alone. It was enough to make Kye leery of ever putting himself back out there again.

Kye waited a few minutes longer before stepping from his office. Aric waited for him, looking unruffled by the encounter. Kye flashed him a grateful smile. "Thank you for that. Working only three days a week has made it a little easier to avoid him, but sometimes he still catches me here."

Aric made a dismissive motion. "No problem. Years of working with men who hate me because of my sexuality has given me the thickest skin imaginable. I have no problem squashing cuddly bear's feelings."

Kye winced at Aric's description. Sonny did look just like a cuddly bear with his full beard and body made for snuggles. "That cuddly bear had no problem squashing my feelings."

Aric nodded, looking serious. "Oh, I'm well aware. That's why he'll never make it past me. No one hurts my friend."

Kye wasn't sure he deserved that title. It always seemed like Aric did more for him than he did for Aric. Kye hugged Aric, and then quickly backed away. He didn't get the impression Aric was much of a hugger. Kye wasn't sure he was either. Probably because no one had touched him in years. Kye's throat unexpectedly swelled. He was tired of being sad.

"Thank you for being my friend. I guess I should go. If I'd left fifteen minutes ago—like I planned to do before I started talking your head off—you wouldn't have had to act as a buffer. Sorry about that. I guess I should man up and just face him." Kye rambled, and he knew it. He didn't know what was wrong with him today. He felt off kilter in a thousand ways.

Aric hugged him, cutting off the nonstop flow of words and putting to rest any concerns Kye had about

Aric's willingness to be hugged. "It's okay. You're not putting me in any weird positions or anything. I'm just glad I was here to help."

Kye took a breath. He was glad too. Usually, Aric spent his days at the office with Baker. This had been one of those days Aric had come home with Baker on his lunch break. He had shown up specifically to hang out with Kye. Now Kye was rushing away. Kye felt worse by the second.

"Will you let me take you to lunch tomorrow? I'm not working then. I could stop by the office and get you, so you don't have to cut into your time driving here."

Aric nodded. "That sounds great. Now get lost before Seth finds some work for you to do."

They made a quick plan for lunch before Kye headed out. With his head down, he barreled toward his BMW, making sure he had all his things while also making mental dinner plans. Cooking for one person always felt pointless. He looked up as he reached his car and found Sonny leaned against his driver's side door. Kye's heart stopped before racing to life again. Sonny had the sweetest brown eyes Kye had ever seen. Before meeting Sonny, Kye hadn't known a person could fake kind eyes.

Kye's steps faltered.

Sonny straightened to his full six-six height. "Hey."

Kye floundered. For a moment, he considered running back inside. He didn't. "Hey." Even to his ears, Kye's tone sounded icy as hell.

Sonny didn't run away the way most men would. "I've been trying to call and catch you here for weeks now. You haven't been answering my calls and you're always gone for the day or... whatever."

Kye almost smiled at Sonny's unwillingness to outright accuse Kye of hiding from him. "I only work part time now."

"Oh." Sonny put his hands in his pockets and immediately removed them. It couldn't have been more obvious he was uncomfortable. "I really just want to explain."

"There's nothing to explain," Kye said, cutting him off. "You had a change of heart or whatever and didn't bother telling me. It happens, I guess." Kye didn't know if that was true. He never dated.

Sonny shook his head. "I didn't change my mind. I panicked. You're you and I'm me. It just didn't seem realistic."

Rage washed over Kye. "Well, I'm so fucking glad standing me up wasn't a big enough insult that you needed to also tell me I'm not good enough for you. Thanks for stopping by."

Sonny's eyebrows snapped together. "What? That's not what I meant at all. I meant there's no way in hell someone as sexy as you would want someone like me. You have a great job and this awesome car. No doubt you live in a huge house and have lots of fancy friends. I'm just a delivery guy who drives a truck and rents a tiny apartment. We don't match."

The insults were piling high. "So, it's not that you're embarrassed of me. You think I'm a snob. I've worked eighteen-hour days, six days a week, for twelve years to have what I do. I came from nothing and worked myself into the ground. You know what? I'm glad you stood me up because I have zero interest in someone who thinks I'm spoiled."

Sonny scrubbed at his face as if Kye drove him crazy. "Fine. All I wanted to do was apologize and see if you'd give me a second chance."

Kye shrugged, feeling spiteful. "Fine. Maybe all I wanted was sex anyhow."

"I can do that."

"Fine," Kye said before he could stop himself. "Text me your address."

Sonny pulled out his phone. "Unblock my number because I'm texting you now. Not that I think you'll show up."

Kye's phone dinged in the front pocket of his scrubs.

Sonny's gaze shot to his.

Kye refused to be embarrassed. "I never blocked your number." Even to his ears, Kye sounded sad. He couldn't help it. Kye had genuinely liked Sonny.

Sonny deflated. "I really am sorry."

Kye didn't know what to say. Sonny's apology sounded genuine. It dawned on Kye that Sonny wasn't wearing his uniform. He looked cute in his jeans and t-shirt. "Are you not working?"

Sonny shook his head. "I'm on vacation this week."

Kye fought a smile. He wasn't ready to forgive Sonny yet, but he had missed their daily chats. "Are you going anywhere—like on a trip?"

"No. I don't have anyone to go places with me and I don't really want to go alone."

It was Kye's turn to shift nervously. He didn't know what else to talk about, but he wasn't ready to give up seeing Sonny's beard-covered face. He had missed Sonny's dark hair and sweet smile. Kye had thought they were friends, if nothing else. He checked his watch. It was one. "It's a little late, but have you had lunch?"

"Yes."

Kye deflated a hair. "Oh. Okay." He couldn't win with Sonny.

"Is that your lunchbox?" Sonny asked, motioning toward the soft insulated bag Kye held.

Kye glanced down at the neoprene bag. "No. It's my insulin. I'm a diabetic. This goes everywhere with me."

"Oh." Sonny's shoulders squared. "Have you had lunch? Because you should definitely have eaten by now if you're diabetic."

A small smile touched Kye's lips. Back when he had constantly fantasized about Sonny, he had always pictured Sonny as protective. He had really wanted this. The disappointment was real. "I was just on my way to grab something."

"Maybe I could take you, then. I could sit with you, so you don't have to eat alone."

Kye opened his car door and threw everything inside, except his insulin. "Okay."

A sweet smile touched Sonny's lips. He motioned toward a large blue F150 parked on the street. "This way." Sonny set his hand on the small of Kye's back and steered him that way.

Kye fought a happy sigh. He didn't know where this was headed or if he would regret this day until he died. It seemed he would soon find out. Kye was too dumb to run for his life. Plus, he wanted this too badly.

·♥·♥·♥·♥·♥·

Sonny was a complete wreck. He hadn't expected Kye to forgive him, much less leave with him. That comment about wanting sex definitely kept rising to the surface. Kye was a million times out of his league. He was tiny, with every muscle perfectly defined. His

Asian descent made his skin look perfectly tanned, and he had these unusual hazel-colored eyes. Kye was fucking beautiful. He had no business being with Sonny. At best, Sonny was a bear. He was a big guy who took up too much space and had too much body hair. In L.A., Sonny was not who gay men wanted. They just didn't match.

The night Sonny had stood up Kye, he had been in full self-destruct mode. He had pictured showing up at Kye's work and everyone laughing at him. It had felt way too good to be true. Now that he had finally gotten to apologize, Sonny saw the truth. He had genuinely hurt Kye's feelings. That fucked with his head. He still couldn't think Kye wanted him. It just couldn't be true. Kye was perfect. It made no sense. Sonny kind of wanted to tell him he was an idiot.

At a tiny cafe near the coast, Sonny watched Kye eat a chicken-topped salad while he tried not to panic. He wanted to ask if Kye had low self-esteem or something. There was no other reason he could come up with to explain why Kye was there with him. The question one hundred percent wouldn't stop beating at his brain. Fuck. Kye was pretty. He had gorgeous lips. Sonny wanted to kiss him again.

"Were you serious about the sex thing?"

"Can I get you another lemon water?" At the server's impeccable timing, heat flooded Sonny's face. He was always a dumbass. That seemed to be doubly true in Kye's company.

A soft and sexy-sounding chuckle floated across the table. Kye's eyes flashed with good humor. "Thank you. I'm sure he'd love a refill."

Sonny fought the urge to cover his face as the server walked away.

Laughter tinged Kye's features. Something inside Sonny melted. He honestly liked Kye. He wanted this to be real. "I'm sorry. I don't know why I always do and say dumb things."

Kye's smile made the confession worthwhile. "Don't apologize. I'm sure that girl has walked into way worse discussions. But to answer your earlier question, no, I wasn't serious about only wanting you for sex. I was just mad." His gaze turned heated as it swept down Sonny's body. "Not that I would turn down sex with you."

Before Sonny could think of a witty retort, their server reappeared with water for Sonny. Sonny sat back and waited until she left to respond. When she walked away, Sonny's mouth ran away without his brain. "You're too beautiful for me."

Laughter flashed in Kye's eyes. "Seriously? Why would you say such a thing?"

There was no way Kye was blind. Sonny absently motioned Kye's way. "Look at you. You're fit and tiny."

He waved toward his body. "I'm like a beached whale over here."

To his surprise, Kye scowled. He looked furious. As quickly as it happened, Kye's expression cleared. He pushed his plate away so he could lean closer. Kye dropped his voice, keeping their conversation quiet. "Do you know what I see? I see a man strong enough to control me. Better than that, I can picture straddling your hips. My hard dick trapped between us. Your gorgeous stomach offering the exact friction needed. I've had that fantasy a thousand times and I can't wait for it to come true."

Sonny's cock leaked with only the picture Kye painted. "Just let me pay the check." Even Sonny heard the arousal in his tone.

Kye smirked. "No hurry. I'm not going anywhere."

Fuck. Sonny had never met anyone like Kye. He was bold, and it was sexy as fuck. Sonny had no clue what he had done right in this life, but he wasn't looking a gift horse in the mouth. Sonny wasn't about hookup culture. Still, he also never paid a check so fast in his life.

Chapter Two

♥

SINCE SONNY ALREADY THOUGHT Kye was out of his league, Kye asked to go back to Sonny's place. No good could come of Sonny seeing his house. Several weeks ago, Kye's boss, Seth, had gifted him with a house after Seth's sister passed. It was a massive estate. Kye was in the process of trying to sell it. There was no way in hell he could pay the taxes and whatnot every year on such a massive place. Still, Sonny would likely die when he saw the place. Sonny didn't realize Kye didn't match his lifestyle. Sometimes even Kye couldn't believe the place belonged to him now. Kye also couldn't handle any more freaking out on Sonny's part. Kye was panicked enough for the both of them.

It had been literal years since Kye fucked anything except toys. There simply hadn't been enough hours in the day. Now Seth had mostly retired, which meant

Kye had all the time in the world on his hands. He was ready to start something real. That didn't mean he wasn't terrified of being a complete failure. It was possible he was about to embarrass the fuck out of himself.

Sonny's apartment was nice. It was manly. Everything was dark with no real style, but the place was clean, and it smelled nice. When Kye toed off his shoes, Sonny grabbed his hand to steady him—like a gentleman. It was sweet. The moment Kye was out of his shoes, Sonny hauled Kye into his arms. The passion was instant. Kye hadn't forgotten that part from the last time they kissed. Sonny's kiss was primal and hungry. He reminded Kye how much smaller Kye was than Sonny. That was not what had Kye trembling. He was nervous as hell and couldn't explain it. There was no way Sonny couldn't feel the way he shook. They were moving fast, and Kye wanted it. Then again, he was a mess and didn't know what he wanted.

Sonny massaged Kye's sides, pushing his shirt higher until he kneaded bare skin. His hands felt rough. Strong. He lifted, leaving Kye with little choice but to wrap his legs around Sonny's waist. Kye felt invaded by the way Sonny's tongue filled his mouth. He loved it. Still, his nerves were on edge. His heart raced so fast, he could barely breathe. Kye couldn't recall the last time he had been so scared. It was stupid, since he had been so bold at the restaurant. Now that it looked like he would have his way, Kye wasn't as sure of himself.

Sonny's kiss gentled as he sat on the couch with Kye straddling his hips. Kye could feel how hard Sonny was for him through his thin scrubs. Only a few scraps of clothing kept Sonny from already being inside him.

Sonny cupped his face and pulled away a hair. "Let's slow down a minute. Why are you shaking?"

Before Kye had time for humiliation to set in, Sonny went back to kissing him. This time, he moved like he had all the time in the world. Kye had forgotten how incredibly sweet Sonny could be. In fact, that was exactly why Kye had been so enamored. He wanted someone nice. Kye wasn't looking for only a hookup. He wanted something real. That was why Kye had to be honest. He leaned away and dropped his forehead to Sonny's shoulder so Sonny wouldn't see his embarrassment.

"I haven't been with anyone in years. I guess I've forgotten how to be... I don't know. Sultry without the humiliation of being completely nude and exposed in every way, I suppose."

Sonny's arms tightened around Kye, holding him closer and warming Kye's heart. He had also forgotten how much he enjoyed being held. A calming breath filled Kye's lungs. He snuggled closer. Sonny was extremely cuddly. Then Sonny kissed Kye's ear. Goosebumps rose on his skin, and his cock jumped.

Sonny did it again. "I like you."

Kye smiled at the confession. He hadn't been this happy in a long time. "I like you too."

More tiny kisses skirted the shell of his ear. Sonny rubbed his back. "There's no hurry. You've definitely got me hard enough to bend steel with my dick, but I can ignore that. This is good too. I've wanted to hold you like this for a long time."

Air filled Kye's lungs, calming him. If Kye was being honest with himself, as much as he wanted sex, he didn't think he wanted it right now. He thought— maybe—what he really sought was intimacy. Not only had Kye not had sex in years, he also hadn't been held in that long. He craved kisses and cuddles. While Kye was willing to trade sex for loving touches, he would rather not just yet.

"I miss being held and kissed."

At Kye's confession, Sonny stood, once again leaving Kye with no other choice than to wrap his legs around

Sonny's waist. Sonny headed down the hall. "Why didn't you say so? I have all the kisses and cuddles you'll ever need."

With his face buried in the crook of Sonny's neck, Kye smiled like an idiot. He was ridiculously happy to be with Sonny. In fact, Kye would say he had never been happier in his life.

·♥·♥·♥·♥·♥·

Even though Sonny had never been hornier in his entire existence, he was beyond relieved he didn't have to take his clothes off yet. He was also bursting with happiness. Sonny didn't date because he had given up on it a long time ago. He wasn't cut out for hookup culture. His stupid heart always got too involved. He always got hurt. Sonny wanted a real relationship. He craved coming home to someone and hearing those three little words so often, he couldn't deny they were true. Sonny wanted to curl up in front of the TV each night, cuddling and stealing kisses. He wanted Kye. There it was. The truth. Kye was the one he pictured in all those fantasies. He was the man of Sonny's dreams.

Sonny knew Kye was out of his league. That didn't stop him from hoping Kye didn't know it. He could make Kye happy. Sonny was a thousand percent positive about that. He just needed to know where to start. Kye had given him a direction to go. Sonny wasn't missing his chance. He carried Kye to bed and gently crawled onto the mattress with Kye in his arms. Once they were settled, Sonny held and kissed Kye, drinking his fill of affection. The hum of arousal was muted and only fueled his emotions. Kye could steal his heart and break it so fucking easily. Sonny couldn't bring himself to care. He wanted this. That meant taking a risk.

"I haven't been with anyone in a long time either," Sonny admitted before he could change his mind.

Kye leaned away enough to meet Sonny's stare. His hazel eyes always took Sonny's breath. He was just so beautiful. It was slightly intimidating. Kye's gaze moved over Sonny's face, as if trying to decide if Sonny was being honest. "You're absolutely gorgeous. Why don't you date?"

Sonny fought a blush. Kye always humbled him with his praise. "Nobody wants to date anymore. They want countless faceless one-night encounters. That's not me. I want something real."

Kye kissed the corner of Sonny's mouth. His breath caught at the sweet gesture. "I want to date you."

The joy that washed over Sonny was immeasurable. He couldn't stop petting Kye and stealing kisses. "Does that mean we're a couple? Like, exclusively?"

Kye's hand found its way beneath Sonny's shirt. He swiped upward, rubbing Sonny's stomach. "I'd like to be."

Sonny couldn't stop smiling. "Good. I'd like to be too."

Kye kissed Sonny's neck. "Then it's settled. You're mine."

Despite his best efforts to forget about his dick, it was getting harder. Kye kept kissing and touching him. Before he knew it, Kye had him on his back, straddling him again. Kye sat back on his heels and ditched his shirt. Sonny stopped breathing. He hadn't been prepared. Kye was even more gorgeous than he expected. Sonny didn't get time to enjoy the show. Kye was back to kissing him. He also worked on stealing Sonny's shirt.

Sonny felt the need to clarify matters again before he got too carried away. "I thought we were cuddling."

Kye nodded. "We are. Let me have your shirt."

Sonny helped Kye peel away his shirt. Kye sat back on his heels again and openly inspected Sonny's bare torso. The hunger in Kye's eyes couldn't be missed. He ran his fingers through Sonny's chest hair.

"Sexy." That was all Kye said before he licked Sonny's nipple.

His cock was definitely jumping and leaking. Sonny wasn't as sure about his ability to ignore it any longer. Kye was killing him. The teasing might break his brain. Kye grabbed the headboard and held himself away. He stared down at Sonny with a heated appreciation Sonny had never witnessed. Sonny wondered then if he would come in his jeans.

"When do you have to go back to work?"

It took Sonny a moment of blinking to fight his way through the lust to find an answer. "Um... Monday is a holiday, so next Tuesday."

Kye ran his fingers through Sonny's chest hair again. "Let me take you on vacation somewhere."

Honestly, all Sonny heard was something about letting Kye take him. "Okay."

A bright smile lit Kye's features. "How do you feel about the mountains? I could see you in some flannel —like a lumberjack."

Sonny truly did not know how to make his brain work with Kye straddling him. "I've never been to the mountains, but it doesn't seem like anyplace would be flannel weather anywhere in the US this time of year."

"Actually, there's a place called Never Summer in Colorado, but I was thinking outside the US."

Kye was thinking way too clearly in Sonny's opinion. "I don't have a passport." Sonny towed Kye down, hoping to steal another kiss. "But if you stayed right here with me, I'd consider it the best vacation spot ever."

With an adorable chuckle, Kye skimmed his lips across Sonny's. "Mhmm, no passport. We'll have to remedy that, but—for now—I need to change fantasies. How about Key Largo? I'd love to steal you away to someplace quiet and hot. You know, so I can get you down to as little clothing as possible."

Fuck. He could have Sonny naked right then if he would quit talking. "Whatever you want. It's yours."

"I have to break my lunch plans with my friend for tomorrow, but I'll make the reservations."

A dam inside Sonny broke. He couldn't take anymore. With a twist and a roll, he had Kye pinned beneath him. The laughter in Kye's eyes told him everything he needed to know. Kye had been waiting for him to break.

·❤·❤·❤·❤·❤·

It was possibly a bit cruel to tease Sonny, considering Kye could feel how hard Sonny was for him. The thing was, Kye needed Sonny to take charge. Kye could be sassy and bold, but he wasn't as sure of himself when it came to dating. They had agreed to be a couple. That should have freed Kye to take his pleasure. It was so much easier to hand over control. Judging by Sonny's expression, he was finished playing.

"You can still say no," Sonny said, between licking Kye's nipples and stealing his pants.

Kye held the headboard and prayed for Sonny to hurry. "That's not happening."

Kye's scrubs were ridiculously easy to peel away. The second he was nude, Sonny's hurried actions slowed. He pressed a kiss to Kye's hipbone. Kye closed his eyes and soaked in the caresses. It was balm on his heart after so long of being alone. He had forgotten how it felt when breaths brushed his skin. Goosebumps ran down his body. Sonny's beard tickled him when Sonny kissed his stomach. Then Sonny licked his crown. Kye's body bowed.

Sonny rolled away and cold air chilled Kye's skin. He was back before Kye opened his eyes and searched for him. Then he heard the crinkle of a condom wrapper. Kye's eyes shot open. He wanted to watch. Kye immediately regretted that decision when he realized everything about Sonny was huge. He couldn't look away. Shy Sonny had disappeared. Aroused Sonny watched Kye with an unmatched heat as he lubed Kye's asshole, stretching him. The hunger made it impossible for Kye to look away. For months, he had craved Sonny. For weeks, he thought they were doomed. He hadn't wanted to give up the dream. Now he was so damn glad Sonny had persisted. This was the guy Kye wanted. He couldn't explain his obsession. There had been this inexplicable draw from the first time Sonny walked into his office. Kye watched his fantasy turn real.

He let go of the headboard and reached for Sonny. Sonny didn't let him down. He settled between Kye's thighs and claimed Kye's mouth. When their bare skin touched and molded, something filled Kye's chest. From nowhere, everything made sense. Kye had met the one. All the days of hoping and flirting had been Kye working toward his future. He genuinely just wanted to be with Sonny. They fit.

Sonny shifted, and his crown pressed against the tight ring of muscles surrounding Kye's asshole. The air changed. Pre-cum smeared across his stomach. His fingers dug into Sonny's skin as Sonny pressed his way inside.

"Fuck."

At Sonny's breathless curse, Kye bit back a moan. Everything about Sonny turned him on. Sonny pushed a little deeper. The air left Kye's lungs. He had never been stretched so wide.

"You're killing me."

Kye thought that was rich, considering he was the one taking a whole lot more dick than he ever expected. Then their gazes met as Sonny slid deeper. It was as if the universe clicked. Emotion clogged Kye's throat. He had never felt closer to anyone. There was zero chance he wouldn't catch feelings. Kye wasn't scared. Everything he felt, he saw reflected back at him. For the first time in his life, Kye understood what people meant when they talked about fate. He knew now why he couldn't get Sonny out of his head. Sonny belonged to him.

Sonny lunged forward and Kye saw stars. The air left his lungs in a whoosh. He sucked in a sharp breath, trying to survive the pleasure. Sonny pulled out a hair and did it again. Kye open-mouth sucked air, trying to get oxygen to his brain. Sonny never looked away from him as he punched that internal button that stole Kye's soul. It was as if all the confidence Sonny lacked in every other aspect of his life manifested as talent in bed. He knew exactly which angle to thrust, and he had no mercy. Kye couldn't focus on anything but the blinding ecstasy. His fingernails tore at Sonny's skin. He wanted everything.

"You're so beautiful."

Kye wanted to return the compliment. His throat wouldn't work for anything other than cries of pleasure.

"I've pictured you beneath me a million times. My imagination isn't as big as I thought. You're a million times hotter underneath me than I ever dreamed."

Fuck. Kye had no clue how Sonny was so coherent while Kye couldn't even suck in a proper breath. Pressure climbed his shaft. It was as if Sonny knew.

"That's it, beautiful. Don't hold back."

Kye swore Sonny coaxed the cum from his cock like a goddamned snake charmer. An orgasm shook Kye's entire body. He couldn't do anything but gasp for air while cum coated his stomach. Sonny pounded inside him. He moaned and cursed, mesmerizing Kye. Sonny threw his head back. The muscles strained in his neck. Kye watched in a pleasure-fueled daze as Sonny came apart. It was the sexiest thing Kye ever witnessed. He knew watching Sonny come would be a porn clip that played in his mind for the rest of his life. It was fucking hot.

Despite his body being completely useless, Kye still hauled Sonny in for a kiss. They both struggled to catch their breath, but that didn't stop their tongues from brushing. Kye's heart did a happy dance. He felt like a new person. Kye couldn't wait to steal Sonny away for the next week. He had no plans on letting Sonny up for air anytime soon. His heart needed more.

Chapter Three

♥

NO MATTER HOW HARD Sonny thought, he couldn't figure out how he ended up floating on a paddle board in Key Largo. Admittedly, he might have agreed to anything when Kye touched him. Fuck. Sonny had never been so damn happy in his life. He couldn't stop staring at Kye paddling nearby. In nothing but a Speedo, Sonny still thought Kye had too many clothes on. He wanted to peel the tiny bathing suit away and eat Kye for dinner. Goddamn, he was obsessed. He was also irritated with the way Kye wouldn't let him pay for anything.

While Sonny imagined Kye meant nothing by it other than being nice, damn. Sonny felt useless. More than that, he couldn't stop holding his breath and waiting for the other shoe to drop. No one was this perfect. Kye looked back over his shoulder and flashed Sonny a smile. Sonny's heart melted. Wow. Kye was really there with him. He couldn't believe it.

"Stop looking at me like that."

At Kye's admonishment, Sonny played dumb. "What? You smiled and I'm just looking at you."

Kye moved his paddle to the other side of his board and steered the board in Sonny's direction. "You know exactly how you're looking at me." He leaned Sonny's way and kissed his shoulder.

Panic raced through Sonny. "Be careful. I don't want you to fall."

Kye's eyes flashed with mischief. "What? You mean like this." In full dramatics, Kye fell into the water.

Sonny's heart tried climbing into his throat. He eyed the water, panicking as Kye didn't resurface. Before he could dive in after him, he was dumped backwards into the water. He came up sputtering and was met by Kye's laughter. Before he could find an ounce of outrage, Kye wrapped himself around Sonny. With their boards blocking them from shore, it felt like they were completely alone in the world. Their faces were inches away. Sonny couldn't tear his gaze away from Kye's gorgeous eyes. Before he could stop himself, Sonny poured his heart out.

"I've never been this happy. That's all on you."

Kye's features softened. "Same. I know you haven't liked me spoiling you this week, but thank you for letting me. You make me want to give you everything. I know you don't have to indulge that."

Honest to God, Sonny had never met anyone like Kye. Their relationship felt very one-sided to Sonny and he didn't know how to make them even. "Tell me how I can spoil you."

A sad smile touched Kye's lips. "You already are. Nobody spends time with me."

Sonny really wanted to ask Kye what he was doing with him. He wasn't that dumb. Sonny wouldn't jeopardize his luck. He kissed Kye instead. If Kye wanted time and attention, Sonny could give him that in droves until Kye got sick of him. Other than working each day, he had nothing else going on. If Kye wanted every free second Sonny owned, he was welcome to them.

Their kiss turned heated.

"We should return these boards and head back to the room."

Sonny completely agreed, except he couldn't move. "If I get out of this water right now, I'm embarrassing us both."

Kye didn't laugh like he hoped. Instead, his gaze dropped to Sonny's mouth, making matters worse. "I'm not embarrassed. Let everyone see I'm wanted."

Fuck. Sonny was in so much trouble. He didn't know if he would make it back to the room.

"Keep an eye out."

Before Sonny could make sense of Kye's words, Kye shoved his hand inside Sonny's swim trunks. Sonny's breath came out in a stuttered gasp. His gaze shot toward the shore. There were only two people, and they were sunning in lounge chairs with their chairs turned away from the water. They were also too far away to see anything Sonny and Kye did. Still, Sonny's eyes burned as he stared at the pair, mentally willing them to stay put.

Sonny released a slow breath as Kye stroked him. He already knew he wouldn't last long. Kye was too much of a temptation. "You're definitely getting your dick sucked when we get back to the room."

Kye made a humming sound at Sonny's promise. "I look forward to it."

Sonny's orgasm built. His gaze slid Kye's way and landed on his sexy mouth. He could picture his cock sliding over Kye's full bottom lip. Fuck. He was so turned on and right on the edge. Every breath he took came faster than the last. He couldn't focus on anything but the pressure climbing his shaft. His gaze shot to the shore again. No one watched them.

Kye kissed his ear.

Ecstasy hit, stealing his breath. His fingers dug into Kye's skin as Kye tugged every drop of pleasure from him.

"Damn. That was sexy. Now I'm the one who has to return these boards with a hard-on."

Sonny claimed Kye's mouth. He was too happy and overwhelmed to think about anything else. Once he caught his breath, he would make Kye fly. For now, he just needed a connection. Sonny was pretty damn sure he had met the love of his life, and it was too damn soon to feel that way. Funny how his heart couldn't tell time. It had never owned a watch.

·♥·♥·♥·♥·♥·

Even though Kye knew they couldn't stay in their little tropical paradise forever, he enjoyed himself way more than he ever imagined. They ate so much food—like ridiculous amounts. There was a small family-owned pizza shop down the road from their hotel that had genuine New York-style pizza, and they couldn't stop going back. When they weren't eating or playing in the water, they were cuddling or making love. Kye didn't want to go home. There was a stupid emotion growing in his chest, and he was trying not to scare Sonny away with it.

"This spot right here has me shook." Sonny kissed Kye's collarbone. "Damn. I'm sorry. I don't know why I can't stop kissing you. You'll probably get sick of me, but I just really want to keep you."

Kye closed his eyes and absorbed Sonny's affection. "I'm down with that. You can put me in your pocket, and I'll ride along with you while you work."

He felt Sonny smile against his skin. "As much as I love the picture you're painting, I'm guessing your patients would miss you."

Kye sighed. "I guess I'll just have to settle for seeing you every night when you get off work." As the words left his lips, Kye wished he could call them back. He sounded needy. Kye held his breath, hoping he didn't ruin things.

Sonny didn't seem fazed. "I like this plan. Every time I think about going home and back to sleeping without you, I feel like I can't breathe. How is it we just started dating? It feels like you've always been mine."

"Just imagine if you'd noticed me sooner."

Sonny tucked Kye against his side and held him. "Oh, I noticed. I've been stopping by your office every day for two years just hoping to catch a glimpse of you. In fact, I can still remember what you were wearing the first day I stopped there. You had on pink scrubs, and you got snippy with me for being late."

Kye laughed. "I did not."

"Uh, huh. It was my first time on a new route, so it took me a little longer. You had been waiting for some paperwork and I threw off your schedule. I thought you would tear the skin off my arm when you ripped the envelope from my hand. But I was still completely enamored. In fact, I rearranged my entire route to make sure I got there earlier the next day, and I brought you a cupcake to apologize."

Fuck. Kye remembered that. He had gotten snippy. "I'm sorry. Back then, Seth had me working myself to death. Every inconvenience was in danger of being the final one."

Sonny kissed the shell of his ear. "Don't apologize. You caught my attention. It took me a long time to figure out if you were interested in men. You never seemed to do anything but work."

Kye made an impatient gesture. "Are you fucking kidding me? I've been flirting with you forever. I didn't think you'd ever notice."

"Honestly? I just thought you were flattering me so I would carry heavy boxes for you."

An outraged snort escaped Kye. "I can't believe you. Do you know I shipped my mom's house keys back to her same-day delivery when she left them in my car just so I could have an excuse to see you?"

A sexy rumble of laughter vibrated against Kye's ear, making him smile. He had never been this happy. A shot of fear hit him in the chest. He didn't want to go back to being alone. If Sonny stopped seeing him, it would hurt worse than Kye was ready to handle. He rolled and buried his face against Sonny's chest. Kye inhaled his scent. He wanted this. Kye would do whatever it took. He was ready to be tied down.

Chapter Four

♥

KYE: *Funny story. Seth didn't even notice my car was in the driveway for the past week.*

Sonny: *He's a newlywed. His brain is elsewhere.*

·♥·♥·♥·♥·♥·

Kye: *I won't be here when you drop off our packages today. I have patients.*

Sonny: *That's too bad. I miss you.*

Kye: *I miss you too. I'll come by when I finish for the day.*

Sonny: *Okay.*

·♥·♥·♥·♥·♥·

Sonny: *I have two more stops and I'll be home.*

Kye: *Yay! I'll pick up dinner. Is that Thai place okay?*

Sonny: *You don't have to take care of dinner every night. I can cook.*

Kye: *I like doing it. It gives you more time to spend with me.*

Sonny: *Even though I don't think I can argue with that, I should make your life easier somehow. If I made you a key, would you take it? That way, you wouldn't have to sit around waiting for me to get off to come over.*

Kye: *If you're okay with me letting myself in, then yeah. I'm okay with that.*

·♥·♥·♥·♥·♥·

Sonny: *Is it weird you have a key to my place, and I've never seen where you live?*

Kye: *I'm not trying to scare you away.*

Sonny: *LOL! You can't scare me.*

Kye: *34561 Low Planes Way.*

Sonny: *Okay. I just Googled that and WTF? Is that your address? Why are you with* me?

Kye: *I told you so.*

Sonny: *I'm not scared. Just WTF?*

Kye: *It's a long story. Basically, Seth gave me the house when his sister passed and I'm trying to sell it.*

Sonny: *That's not a house. That's a VILLAGE!*

·♥·♥·♥·♥·♥·

Sonny: *Did I piss you off? You're not texting me.*

Kye: *Sorry. I had a patient. Are you still mad about the house I didn't earn?*

Sonny: *I'm not mad. I just don't know how to be worthy of you.*

·♥·♥·♥·♥·♥·

I'm not mad. I just don't know how to be worthy of you. That text ran through Kye's mind on repeat all day. He had kept Sonny away from his place for three months because he had known Sonny would react like this. Kye had no clue why Sonny was so certain Kye was out of his league. It wasn't true. They were a matching set, as far as Kye was concerned. Sonny made him happy. He hoped he made Sonny happy. End of story. Apparently, that wasn't the end of the story to Sonny.

Kye drove to Sonny's place on autopilot. His mind raced with ways to make Sonny understand how much he meant. By the time he pulled into a parking spot outside Sonny's apartment, Kye was more confused than ever. If he did anything, Sonny would just see it as Kye pulling ahead of him in this imaginary contest. Kye had been out of the dating pool too long. He had no clue what he was doing. Kye sat there much longer than he intended, trying to figure things out.

His car door opened, and Sonny squatted down beside him. "Are you planning to sit in the car all night?"

Kye looked his way, feeling defeated. He loved seeing Sonny's sweet face. Kye just wasn't sure Sonny would ever feel the same. "You're not really happy with me, are you?"

A line appeared between Sonny's eyebrows. "What in the hell are you talking about? Of course I am."

Kye's chest hurt. "Then I don't understand why you're always looking for the barriers between us. I thought we were happy. Why does it matter so much where I live or who picks up dinner? I just want to be with you. Why isn't that enough?"

Sonny's expression cleared and then closed. He reached inside the car and unsnapped Kye's seatbelt. "Grab what you need, baby."

Kye grabbed his insulin bag and Sonny lifted him from the car like a baby. With Kye cradled to his chest, he hip-checked the door closed and headed inside. Sonny looked way too serious for Kye's comfort, but damn. They couldn't keep pretending Sonny didn't like certain things about Kye, and Kye couldn't apologize for being himself.

Once they were closed inside the house, Sonny carried Kye to the kitchen so he could drop off his insulin. Then he headed straight for bed.

After setting him on the bed, Sonny took off Kye's shoes and unloaded his pockets. Once he had Kye comfortable, Sonny tackled Kye to the bed and cuddled him—hard.

"I have something I need to say," Sonny said against his ear after a few minutes.

Kye nodded, his throat tight. He had never been more frightened in his life. Kye didn't want to lose Sonny.

"I'm sorry I made you feel like I saw barriers between us at every turn. That's not the problem. Not really."

Since Kye hadn't been aware they had a problem, he was already on the verge of tears. "Then what is wrong?"

"I'm scared as fuck of losing you," Sonny said, surprising him. "It's possible I am pointing out every little thing, trying to decide why you want me. I guess I'm trying to point things out before you realize them for yourself and leave. It's stupid, I know. It's already too late to avoid getting my heart broken. If I lost you, it would kill me."

Aggravation grew inside Kye, trying to crush his brain. "Why do you feel that way, though? I'm not going anywhere. I don't want to break your heart," Kye said, huffing in his frustration. "I love you. All I'm trying to do is love you." He felt Sonny go still, as if he held his breath. Kye realized too late what he had admitted.

After a heartbeat passed, Sonny's muscles relaxed, and he released his breath. "I love you too. You're all I want."

A small smile tugged at Kye's lips. "Maybe you could stop fighting me at every turn, then. I like handling dinner and I didn't earn that house."

Sonny smiled. "Maybe you could kiss me hello instead of accusing me of being unhappy."

Kye's smile grew. He hadn't really expected Sonny would ever love him. That was... wow. Kye fingered the collar of Sonny's shirt and lured him down. He bumped noses with Sonny before whisking his lips across Sonny's. Happiness grew in his chest as reality settled in. Sonny loved him. This was his person. He would never be alone again. Sonny wouldn't let him hurt. He was making a big deal out of nothing. This was real. Wow.

·❤·❤·💛·❤·❤·

Sonny couldn't stop kissing Kye or smiling. Damn. He hadn't expected the night to go this way. Everything had been a bit of a blur since he Googled that address. Sonny had not expected a multimillion-dollar home to pop up on his phone. That had nearly taken him out. He had already known Kye was way out of his league. It had been a really humbling moment to see that house.

Then Kye had shown up, looking defeated. Until that moment, Sonny hadn't truly considered how his reaction affected Kye. He had thought Kye so far above him, Sonny hadn't realized he could hurt Kye at all. Then he had seen how he slowly poisoned them, crushing the life from their beautiful relationship with his bullshit. He didn't know why Kye loved him, but he did. Sonny couldn't squash the happiness. He had found the one.

For close to an hour, they cuddled and kissed before moving to the shower. With hot water running down their bodies, Sonny soaped Kye's skin. He scrubbed every place he could reach. Sonny took care of his angel the way Kye deserved. He washed Kye's hair, gently massaging the shampoo into every strand. Every few seconds, he stole Kye's kisses. His body burned, but it was nothing compared to the fire inside his heart. This was love. Sonny couldn't get enough.

With their bodies clean, Sonny dried Kye's skin before wrapping him in a fluffy towel. He carried Kye to bed. Nude and still damp, they cuddled and kissed. There was no rush to do anything. They simply enjoyed their newfound freedom to speak freely about their feelings. Sonny told Kye he loved him so many times, he wondered if Kye was sick of him yet. Each and every time, Kye returned the words. Not a hint of annoyance marred his features. Sonny was in heaven.

Just as things heated up, Kye's phone rang. Sonny snagged it from the bedside table, passed it along, and kept kissing every place he could reach.

Kye put the phone on speaker and answered while still writhing beneath Sonny's touch. "Hello?"

His breathless tone had Sonny smiling against his skin. A female's voice came through the line, speaking heavy and fast Japanese. Sonny tuned it out while he kissed Kye's throat.

Kye turned his chin up, giving Sonny better access. "You know I work, Momma."

Sonny's hand slipped beneath the covers. He heard his name in the middle of the fast rant. He froze. Kye grabbed his hand and helped Sonny back on track by wrapping Sonny's fingers around his cock. Sonny was effectively distracted again.

"I'll ask him later and let you know."

Sonny kissed a path down Kye's chest. Kye sucked in a sharp breath. Sonny smiled against Kye's stomach as he moved lower.

"I love you, Momma. I've got to go now." Kye disconnected the call and buried his fingers in Sonny's hair as Sonny wrapped his lips around Kye's cock. He sucked. Kye moaned. Sonny fell into a rhythm, bobbing on Kye's erection. Obviously losing patience, Kye shoved at Sonny's chest until he had Sonny on his back. Sonny watched as Kye rolled a condom down Sonny's length. He squirted lube everywhere and sat on Sonny's dick. .

Sonny gasped for air.

Kye showed him no mercy. He lifted and sat, riding Sonny's cock. All Sonny could do was stroke Kye's erection and hope he brought Kye half the pleasure Kye gave him. The tight heat squeezing Sonny's dick drove him wild. He thrust upward, matching Kye's pace. Sonny tried getting deeper. He wanted to connect with Kye's soul. Kye leaned back and fucked Sonny's palm as he ground down on Sonny's cock.

With his head thrown back, Kye took his pleasure. Cum hit Sonny's chest and Kye's asshole clamped tight on Sonny's dick. Sonny saw stars as Kye pulled him over the edge. Cries tore from his throat as spasms shook him. They were beautiful together. Nothing could break them.

Chapter Five

♥

KYE: *I LOVE YOU.*

Sonny: *I love you too. How's your day going?*

Kye: *Meh. I keep forgetting to tell you that my mom wants us to come for dinner one night.*

Sonny: *That's fine. Just pick a night and we'll go.*

Kye: *Are you sure? I don't want to rush you.*

Sonny: *Baby, you couldn't rush me. Never. Not in any way. I'm in this for as long as you'll have me and in any capacity that you'll have me. Just set up the dinner.*

Kye: *Okay. I love you.*

Sonny*: I love you too.*

·♥ · ♥ · ♥·♥·♥·

Kye*: I have a problem.*

Seth: *What's up?*

Kye: *Sonny and I are having dinner with my parents tonight.*

Seth: *Fuck.*

Kye: *Yeah.*

Seth: *Did you warn him they're assholes?*

Kye: *Do you think I should? They might behave. I told them to behave.*

Seth: *More likely they'll just be assholes in Japanese.*

Kye: *True. I should be good then, right?*

Seth: *Yeah. You should be good.*

· ♥ · ♥ · ♥ · ♥ · ♥ ·

Gah. Sonny couldn't be happier. Every time Kye texted him a random message, telling him he loved him, Sonny melted a little more inside. He didn't know where to go with so much love. That didn't stop his insides from shaking as they drove to Kye's parents' house for dinner. Kye had put them off for a while. He claimed he wanted to save Sonny from being interrogated. Sonny fought his insecurities that told him it was something more than that.

Thankfully, their house looked like a normal home. It was a three-bedroom vinyl siding home in a middle-class neighborhood. The place looked a lot like the home Sonny had been raised in. That gave Sonny some hope they could find common ground. Oddly enough, Sonny's biggest fears had to do with race. He recognized Kye's parents might not want a white man for their son. To be safe, and for almost the entire six months they had been dating, Sonny had been slowly learning Japanese. He listened to audiobooks while he worked, and he played games on his phone that helped teach languages. Sonny didn't know enough to hold conversations, but he could understand words when spoken. He hoped this helped in some small way.

Ena and Kenji were all smiles as they met Kye and Sonny at the door. Kye's mom, Ena, hugged Sonny as he stepped inside. She was the one who gave Kye his hazel eyes. Sonny wanted to like her for that reason alone. Kenji was a bit more reserved, and looked nothing like Kye, but he welcomed Sonny to his home. They spoke to him in English, but only in Japanese to each other. His lessons helped. Unfortunately, he learned nothing good. Mostly, he gathered they had been expecting him to be a girly boy. At least he wasn't that. That was the point he decided to keep his understanding of the language to himself.

The dinner conversation was awkward and stilted, but everyone smiled uncomfortably a lot. Sonny wasn't very good at meeting new people. Kye kept squeezing his knee beneath the table, as if trying to lend him strength while Sonny explained his job and how he had met their son.

"He's not eating my food."

Sonny took a bite while still trying to pretend he didn't understand anything they said.

"He's a big boy. Maybe he should eat less."

Sonny set his fork aside and focused on Kye.

Kye was scowling at his plate. "Stop it and stop speaking in Japanese. You're being rude." Kye squeezed his knee again.

Sonny could see the tension in Kye's shoulders. Something inside him snapped. *"You have a nice home."* Sonny spoke slowly in Japanese, so they would know he wasn't very good at speaking their language, but he could understand them.

A sharp bark of laughter burst from Kye.

His parents looked horrified.

Ena cleared her throat. "Thank you. Kenji has worked many years for it."

Everyone collectively took a drink, as if this couldn't be done soon enough. By the time dinner was over, Sonny was ready to run for the car. He wondered if Kye would dump him in the car on the way home or if he would wait until they made it back to where Kye's car waited for them at Sonny's apartment, so he could make a clean getaway.

Sonny stood feet away on the sidewalk and listened to their goodbyes. He felt like an idiot. This was miserable. No doubt Ena and Kenji were every bit as relieved it was over. Unfortunately, Sonny got the feeling his relationship was also over.

Then the front door closed, leaving them alone. Kye turned his way with laughter flashing in his eyes. "You know Japanese. That's fucking hilarious. My parents will never, ever forget that."

Sonny covered his face. "I can't believe that happened. I'm so sorry. I've been slowly learning the language for you. That was horrible. I'm sorry."

Kye pulled Sonny's hands away from his face and dragged him toward the truck. "Please. They had it coming." He wrapped his arms around Sonny's bicep. "I should've warned you they're jerks. That's on me. I really hoped they would behave, since Mom knows how I feel about you. I'm sorry they're awful."

Sonny ran through the night in his head as he backed Kye against the passenger side of his truck. "I don't know. It didn't go completely horrible. I also learned your mom thinks I have nice eyes, and your dad is happy I don't look gay."

Kye's entire body shook with laughter. "I'm sorry. I know it's not funny. It's just that I've never seen them contrite. That was impressive."

The more Sonny thought about it, the more humor he found in the situation. Plus, Kye looked happy. That was all that mattered to Sonny. "So I impress you. Now I'm wondering how I can exploit this knowledge."

Kye's laughter died away as his expression turned heated. He held Sonny's stare as he wrapped his arms around Sonny's neck. "Name your price. I'm your willing captive."

Rather than ask for anything, Sonny kissed him. The night might not have gone the way Sonny hoped, but they were still strong. Sonny couldn't ask for more.

·♥·♥·♥·♥·♥·

Sonny had learned Japanese for him. Fuck. Kye couldn't get over it. Every time he thought he couldn't fall more in love with Sonny, he did. Kye had genuinely believed this night would be a disaster. While—in some ways—he had been right, Sonny had proven to be more amazing than any problem they might face. It felt like a total win to Kye. Kye decided it was time to go out on a limb with something he had already set in motion.

"Do you mind if we make a quick stop before we go back to your place?"

Sonny looked beyond curious. "Not at all. Where are we headed?"

Kye shook his head. "It's a surprise. You drive and I'll point the way."

"All right." Sonny brushed another quick kiss across Kye's lips and then helped him into the truck.

Once Sonny was behind the wheel, Kye gave Sonny directions while nervousness ate at the lining of his stomach. He kind of wondered if he would be sick. When they pulled into a driveway—in a nice neighborhood and halfway between their workplaces —Sonny looked his way with raised eyebrows.

Kye flashed him a smile and jumped from the truck. He waited for Sonny to join him. Then, hand in hand, they headed for the door. Kye typed in a code on the front door's lock, and the doorknob easily turned beneath his hand. He walked backward into the empty house.

Sonny looked around. "What is this place?"

Kye's shoulders expanded as he took a deep breath. "It's the house I just bought... for us."

Sonny didn't react. For a moment, he stared at Kye in silence. "You bought a house for us?"

He didn't sound thrilled. Kye's confidence shook. "Yeah. I mean, the house Seth gave me sold a few days ago and this place is halfway between your work and mine. It's a new build, in a good neighborhood. A great school zone."

"School zone," Sonny repeated, looking more closed by the second.

Suddenly, Kye didn't feel quite so positive about his purchase. "Yeah. You don't like it." Kye had never been more positive of anything in his life.

Sonny's expression didn't change. "It's not that. Obviously, you're free to do as you want with your money, but you just bought a house... for us. We hadn't talked about that yet."

That was true. Kye had assumed they were on the same page with where this relationship was headed. They had been exchanging I love yous and spending every night together. Sonny had learned Japanese for him. Kye didn't think he was that far out there with his plan. Yet it was beyond obvious Sonny didn't want this.

"Oh. Well. I mean, you don't have to move in with me right now. I just thought... never mind. It's no big deal. I guess, this is where I'll be living soon." Kye made a wide dismissive gesture toward the room in general.

Sonny nodded. "It's nice."

Kye genuinely thought he might vomit. "I guess we should go, since I don't have any furniture here yet. There's no place for us to sit or anything."

"You can show me around."

Kye shook his head, hoping he didn't cry. "It's fine. When I get my things moved in, we'll come back."

It was obvious Sonny tried to brush off Kye's misstep. "If that's what you want."

Kye nodded and steered Sonny outside.

As he reset the lock, Sonny crowded his space. "It's a really nice place."

Kye didn't respond. He was a little scared of his voice at that moment. For the life of him, he couldn't understand how he had been so wrong about them. Having shitty parents probably didn't help. Kye tried not to think about the way Sonny had been treated at dinner. Who would want to tie themselves to that?

They rode back to Sonny's place in silence. Sonny kept taking his hand and kissing it, but the pains in Kye's chest wouldn't stop. He felt like an idiot. Kye had jumped the gun tonight, but he had genuinely believed he had done something special for them. He had truly thought he would marry Sonny someday. Now all his plans sounded crazy, even to him. What had he been thinking, buying them a house without talking to Sonny first?

A hint of anger wormed its way inside Kye's hurt. He had been thinking they were headed somewhere. Kye wasn't wrong for that. Any sane person would feel the same… unless he was genuinely just a piece of ass to Sonny. Maybe Sonny liked things the way they were because he had an out. At any time, he could decide he was done. Well, maybe Kye was done.

They pulled into the parking lot of Sonny's apartments. Kye got out without waiting for Sonny. He pulled his keys from his pocket and headed for his car. Sonny was hot on his heels.

"Where are you going?"

There was a hint of laughter in Sonny's voice, feeding Kye's anger. Still, he tried to make light of things. "I'm crazy tired. Dealing with my parents is exhausting. I think I'll just head home."

A line appeared between Sonny's eyebrows. "Are you sure? I was kind of under the impression we needed to talk."

Kye held Sonny's stare, daring him to say more. "Why would we need to talk?"

Sonny shifted from one foot to the other. He shook his head. "I guess I'm worrying about nothing." He closed the space between them and kissed Kye. Kye melted for half a second. Then he remembered Sonny didn't want him forever. Kye climbed into his car and didn't look back. Halfway home, he realized it was the first time he left without Sonny telling him he loved him since they exchanged that first I love you. That was when the first tear fell.

Chapter Six

❤

SONNY: *You didn't text me when you got home and you're not answering my calls. Do I need to call the police or did you make it home okay?*

Kye: *Sorry. I'm good. I'm seeing patients today.*

Sonny: *Okay. I love you.*

·❤·❤·❤·❤·❤·

Sonny: *Okay. It's been three days of unanswered texts, and you're never in the office when I stop by. I get that I'm being ignored, but why?*

·♥·♥·♥·♥·♥·

Sonny: *Jesus. I told you we needed to talk before you left my place last Tuesday. You acted like we were fine. We're obviously not fine. Please talk to me.*

Sonny: *I love you and I'm sorry. The house is perfect. I'd live with you anywhere. You just caught me off guard.*

·♥·♥·♥·♥·♥·

Sonny: *Please talk to me.*

Okay. He had fucked up. Sonny completely got that, but he didn't know what to do. He didn't know where to turn. Kye wasn't answering his texts, and he wasn't at the office when Sonny stopped by there for deliveries each day. The crazy huge house had been sold, so Sonny knew Kye wasn't living there. The house he had bought for them was still empty and now had a for sale sign in the yard. Sonny was at a loss and heartbroken. It was worse because he knew it was his fault.

He couldn't explain why he had freaked. It was just that Kye was all these amazing things and Sonny was nothing. If Sonny let Kye buy them a house, then that was one more way he didn't measure up. Kye didn't see it, but he would wake up one day and realize that their relationship was eighty-twenty. He would resent the fuck out of Sonny when that day came. All Sonny knew to do now was to try the same tactic he had the last time Kye stopped talking to him. He took the day off to stalk Kye.

Unfortunately, unlike last time, Kye's car wasn't in the driveway at the house where he worked. Still, Sonny went inside—like he had every right to be there. Even though Sonny knew—technically—the place was Kye's boss's house, it was the only lead he had. As he came through the door, the tall blond doctor who Kye worked for stood behind the wooden counter that separated Kye's office from the foyer. He looked up as Sonny came through the door.

"If you're looking for Kye, he's not in today."

Sonny nodded. "I didn't see his car out there, but I still hoped you could help me."

Seth's expression looked unreadable. Sonny had always thought of him as being a bit cool. It made Sonny wonder at his bedside manner, but judging by the size of his house, people obviously loved him as their physician. "What can I do for you?"

Sonny decided to be honest and hope for the best. "I fucked up with Kye. He bought us a house without talking to me first and I freaked a little. Now he's not talking to me, and I don't even know where he's living at the moment."

Seth blinked. If he felt one way or the other about Sonny's spiel, he didn't show it. He tapped the papers in his hand on the counter and stapled them together. "You're dating someone, and you don't know where they live."

It was Sonny's turn to blink. "Yeah. I mean, everything happened all at once. He sold the house you gave him, bought another, and now it's up for sale. I gather he meant the new house to be a surprise, so he didn't tell me the other house had sold or where he was staying in the interim. I thought he was still at the house you gave him."

Seth still showed no reaction. "Do you not stay the night with him sometimes?"

Sonny rubbed the back of his neck. "Not really, no."

"Why?"

Seth's emotionless responses were kicking Sonny's ass. "He just always stays with me."

"Why?"

Sonny was seriously on the edge of snapping. "Look, I don't know. I get off work later than him, so he always comes to me."

"I'm not trying to be an ass," Seth said, sounding calm in the face of Sonny's hysteria. "I'm just confused, so let me see if I've got this straight. Kye always comes to you despite obviously having to sit around all day waiting for you to get home. Then he bought you a house so he wouldn't have to sit around in a strange apartment all day, waiting for you to get home, and you freaked about that. I feel like I'm missing something. What the hell did you freak about? It sounds like you had it made."

Sonny pinched the spot between his eyes where a pain bloomed. "Yeah. I'm aware. Could you at least tell Kye I'm looking for him?"

"Sure."

With Seth's agreement in place, Sonny left. It was obvious Seth wouldn't help him. The only trick he had left up his sleeve was Kye's parents, and Sonny dreaded the fuck out of that.

·♥·♥·♥·♥·♥·

The four walls of Kye's office were getting smaller every day. Until recently, he hadn't notice how bare the cream-colored surfaces really were. Other than his degrees, nothing marred the walls. Since the night he had driven away from Sonny without looking back, Kye kept his door shut while he was at work. Kye also no longer parked out front. Instead, he kept his car in Seth's garage, and he left a box on the counter for outgoing and incoming packages. Kye took no chances when it came to accidentally running into Sonny. They were done.

Seth opened Kye's office door without knocking and wandered inside. He looked confused as hell. "You just had a visitor."

Kye dropped his gaze to the paperwork on his desk to hide the pain blooming in his chest. "Is that so?"

Seth didn't leave or back down at Kye's unwelcoming tone. "Yeah. Do you want to tell me what's going on? I know you've told everyone not to let Sonny know where you are, but that guy looks genuinely hurt. So, spill."

For a moment, Kye considered telling Seth everything. He needed a friendly ear. The problem was Kye still hurt too bad. He didn't want to talk about how wrong he had been about their relationship. It meant less than nothing that Sonny came looking for him. They had been together six months with little to no effort from Sonny. What did it matter now?

"I love you, but I really can't do this, okay?"

For a moment, Seth didn't respond. Finally, he set some paperwork on Kye's desk and let it go. "Okay, but if you change your mind, you know where I am."

With his head down, Kye nodded. He appreciated Seth, but everything cut too deeply at the moment. When he was alone again, Kye rubbed his chest. He'd had way too much time to think since driving away from Sonny and anger had taken hold. Everything Kye had done for Sonny still made sense to him. He regretted nothing, because the fact that they were so easy was what he loved so much about them. They didn't fight. They just existed peacefully together and had fallen in love quietly. That was exactly why Kye hadn't thought twice about buying them a house. He had expected to keep flowing forward without issue.

Now Kye realized they weren't flowing peacefully forward. Kye was carrying them, and he hadn't noticed the weight of it because he always fucking carried everyone. He had spent twelve years working himself into the ground for Seth. It was only the last two years he had recognized his exhaustion. That meant he had happily killed himself for ten years without notice. He realized now he had done the same with Sonny. Kye rubbed his chest again. He likely would have carried them forever if Sonny had let him, because he hadn't been unhappy. Kye had loved being there when Sonny got home. He adored having dinner waiting and getting all the snuggles. Most of all, Kye had lived for knowing Sonny felt the same way. The thing was, Sonny didn't feel the same, and Kye knew it now. He couldn't un-know it, and that broke him.

The chime sounded again at the front door, and Kye swallowed a groan. Seth hadn't shut his office door, and no one was there to run interference if Sonny had returned. All Kye could do was hope Sonny wouldn't circle the counter and find him there.

"Hello?"

Kye scowled. It didn't sound like Sonny.

"Yes?" Even to Kye's ears, he sounded uncertain.

A bald head popped around the counter. "Oh, hi."

Kye smiled at the shy greeting. "Sorry. I was doing paperwork." He stood and circled his desk. "How can I help you?"

The guy smiled. His blue eyes flashed with good humor. "I'm looking for Kye Nakada."

"That's me."

The guy visibly tried to switch to business mode, but he still looked too friendly for his own good. "Oh, hey. I'm Steven. There's a couple seriously interested in buying your house, but my boss, Clive Sampson, hasn't been able to get ahold of you."

Kye fought a wave of sadness. "Sorry about that." He hadn't thought about his realtor not being able to reach him when he turned off his phone almost a week earlier. "I turned my phone off for... reasons." Kye didn't know what else to say. He didn't think it was necessary to explain himself.

Steven's smile turned kind. He pushed his glasses up his nose as Kye moved closer. Kye didn't miss the way he tried to check Kye out on the sly. Kye fought a smile. He felt like shit, and he didn't want attention, but it was nice to know someone looked twice.

Silence grew between them. Kye had to break it. "If you want to leave the offer with me, I'll look it over and get back to you."

Steven visibly shook himself. "Yeah. The offer. Sorry. You have gorgeous eyes. Sorry. I really shouldn't have said that."

Kye smiled. There was no happiness behind it. Everything sucked. He hurt. "Thank you. That was a compliment I needed today."

Steven frowned. "Are you okay?"

Kye nodded. "I will be." He just needed a few bottles of wine and a night under the roof he had planned to share with Sonny. After that, he would accept the offer on his new house, no matter what it was. Even if he took a loss, it wouldn't be the worst thing to happen to him lately. But maybe he could move on.

Chapter Seven

♥

THE FRONT DOOR TO the house Kye had bought for them stood open and Kye's car was in the driveway. Thank God Sonny had decided to drive by one final time. Sonny damn near hit the ground running before his truck stopped rolling. Even though he would have stalked Kye forever, he was ridiculously relieved that an entire day of relentless pursuit had finally panned out. He couldn't get to Kye fast enough.

As he peeked inside the house, Sonny's heart leaped into his throat. Kye was on the living room floor. Sonny rushed inside without knocking. He damn near doubled over with relief when he saw Kye was alive. There were two open bottles of wine next to him. Kye stared at the ceiling. He barely reacted at the sight of Sonny.

Sonny sat next to him on the floor. "I've been looking for you."

Kye didn't respond.

Sonny realized Kye's nose and eyes were red, as if he had been crying. His heart sank. "So, you're really done with me, huh?"

He wished Kye would say something, but he didn't. Sonny turned and settled onto his back next to Kye.

"This was supposed to be our ceiling."

Sonny's eyes stung at Kye's quiet words. "It still could be."

"No. I sold it. At a forty-thousand-dollar loss since I just bought the place."

Sonny's eyes fell closed. "I don't have that much in my savings, but you can have it. I get that it doesn't make up for anything."

Kye sat up and took a drink. He angrily set the bottle aside. "I don't fucking get it. Like what is it about me that makes everyone say, 'Here's some money. I know it doesn't make up for completely overlooking everything you've done for me, but you're good now, right?' That's how I ended up with Seth's sister's house, and now you think your life savings will fix everything. You know what? Fuck you both." He took another angry swig.

"I love you."

Kye didn't respond.

Sonny didn't give up. "I knew this would happen. I knew you'd wake up one day and realize you gave more than me. That's why I panicked when you bought this house. How am I supposed to treat you the way you deserve when I could never buy you a place like this?"

Kye stood. He stumbled a bit as he grabbed his wine bottles, but he didn't let it slow him. "You tell me, Sonny. What could you have possibly done to compete? Maybe," he said, waving the bottles wildly. "Just maybe it wasn't a fucking competition. Perhaps, and this is just wild conjecture on my part, but it's possible I just wanted you to fucking love me. That was it. Dumb, I know, but lesson learned." Kye's shoulders fell. He headed for the door.

Sonny jumped to his feet. "Where are you going?"

Kye polished off the second bottle of wine and dumped them in the trash can outside. "I'm going back to sleep under my boss's roof where I've been living for months now and will likely live until I die, seeing as no one wants me."

Sonny scrubbed at his forehead. "I want you, and if you think you're fucking driving out of here, you've lost your goddamn mind."

Kye looked up at the sky, took a breath, and dropped. In his shock, Sonny didn't react right away. Then Kye didn't move. It hit Sonny something was really wrong. Sonny raced to his side. He was out and breathing too fast. Sonny called nine-one-one while making all the promises. If Kye would just be okay, then Sonny would be the best husband Kye had ever seen because they were one thousand percent getting married and living wherever Kye chose. In fact, Sonny was never leaving Kye's side again. Kye wouldn't even be going to the bathroom alone. There was nothing he wouldn't do. He just needed Kye to be okay.

· ♥ · ♥ · ♥ · ♥ · ♥ ·

One of the things that sucked severely about diabetes was the effects of over-drinking. Since that was something Kye never did, he hadn't realized he would experience a sudden change in heart rhythm that would completely take him out. His subsequent trip to the ER and hangover were price enough for him, but not for karma, it seemed. He was also in Sonny's bed with no phone, car, or way to escape. Plus, Sonny was angry as hell with him. Not that it mattered, since they were over. But Kye felt too bad to figure out how to get home, and Sonny wouldn't stop glowering at him.

"You can take me home."

Sonny's frown grew darker at Kye's glib tone. "You are home."

A sigh gathered in Kye's throat. He refused to let it fly. "I don't have my phone."

"You haven't answered a call in days and now you're worried about your phone."

Kye fought hard against an eye roll. "How long do you plan to stay mad at me?"

"I haven't decided. You need to eat something."

Kye eyed the insulin pen and plate of food Sonny had set on the table next to the bed for him thirty minutes ago. His stomach churned at the idea of chewing.

With a huff, Sonny grabbed Kye's plate and insulin and climbed into bed next to him. He jabbed Kye with the pen before Kye saw it coming. Then he tore Kye's toast into tiny bites and held a piece out to Kye. "It's too late. You've had your shot. Eat."

Kye dutifully opened his mouth. He knew from experience he couldn't wait longer than fifteen minutes after his shot to eat, so there was no sense in throwing a fit. Kye already felt bad enough.

"Your eggs are cold, but that's your own damn fault."

Kye opened his mouth and let Sonny feed him the cold eggs because he didn't like the way he felt when Sonny was mad at him. After a few minutes of eating, some of the anger bled from Sonny's features.

"You really piss me off," Sonny said from nowhere, as if he couldn't hold it in any longer.

Kye pulled the blanket higher and twisted.

Sonny's gaze dropped to the motion. He took a few breaths and went back to feeding Kye. Sonny visibly tried to stay calm when he spoke again. "What do you think is the worst thing that could've happened if you had just said, 'I bought us this house and we're living in it, so get the fuck over yourself?' What do you think would've happened?"

Kye shrugged. "I guess you could've told me you didn't see yourself with me for the rest of your life and completely crushed my soul."

Sonny stared at him in silence for a moment, as if waiting for Kye to come to some conclusion on his own. When it didn't happen, Sonny set the plate aside. "So, you chose instead to crush me first, right?"

Kye shook his head. "You obviously don't want me forever, so I moved along and tried to save myself."

Sonny looked as if he fought not to say all the words. He took an audible breath like he tried not to tear into Kye. "I know that I can be pretty dumb, but I also know that you know I want you forever."

Sonny could say what he wanted, but some facts still remained. "If you wanted me, you would've been thrilled with that house. You looked at me like you couldn't believe I had the audacity to think you would bother spending the rest of your life with me. How was I supposed to feel? How was I supposed to react?" Kye shook his head, getting really upset. "I thought you were the one. I would've done anything for you."

"Except talk to me, I guess," Sonny said, sounding defeated.

Kye wasn't loving this. He didn't like to fight, but he wouldn't back down now. "Okay. Talk. Tell me how horrible I am for trying to share my life with you. I can take it."

Rather than give Kye the fight he looked for, Sonny just looked sad. "You'll never know how much I wish I had reacted differently. I wish I would've jumped up and down and ran from room to room, checking out our new house. At least, if I had faked it for a moment, you wouldn't be questioning my love now. But the thing is, I knew the day would come when you realized you're too good for me. And that's exactly what happened the second I didn't pretend to be happy about you spending a—no doubt—ridiculous amount of money on a house without letting me try to help, even if only with the down payment. We both know I don't make as much as you do. It's beyond obvious I'm not what gay men are looking for here in

L.A. Everyone who looks at us knows you're too good for me. So I don't think I'm being ridiculous for wanting to take part in building a life with you. Otherwise, it's just your life and I'm a visitor. I don't want to be just a fucking guest, Kye. I love you. I want to spend the rest of my life *with* you. Not underneath you. Well, I would definitely spend my life underneath, underneath you, but you get the gist of what I'm saying. I want to be your partner in life. Not your pet."

Despite himself and everything else, Kye caught himself smiling. "I like having you, beneath me, beneath me, but not below me. So I get it." He wouldn't like it if he felt like he was just a guest in Sonny's life. Kye never meant to make Sonny feel that way. He had just gotten carried away. Kye's shoulders fell. "But that house."

Sonny pulled a pained face. "It is pretty awesome. I could definitely picture us living there."

Excitement blindsided Kye. This was the happiness he had wanted to share with Sonny when he found that house for them. "Right? It had the perfect spot for a pool and the backyard already had a privacy fence. There was a built-in grill out back."

Sonny looked thoughtful. "I could probably afford to get us a pool built." He shook his head. "I'm not going there. It's gone already. We'll find another place."

Kye chewed his bottom lip. "I haven't actually signed anything yet. I'm not legally bound to sell the house."

Sonny spent a moment eyeing Kye. Then he stood, crossed the room, and grabbed something from the dresser before returning to Kye's side. He looked uncomfortable. "Before everything went to hell, I was waiting for the right time. Now I realize there's no time like the present because I can't lose you." Sonny sat on the bed and held out a ring box to Kye.

With his heart in his throat, Kye opened the box. His gaze lifted. Sonny looked as if he held his breath. "What's this?"

"It's wedding bands."

"Are you…"

Sonny nodded. "Will you marry me?"

Kye lunged forward and tackled Sonny to the bed. His nausea didn't magically disappear, but happiness eclipsed everything.

Sonny stroked his back. "Is that a yes?"

Kye nodded, trying not cry. "Yes."

Sonny rolled and pinned Kye to the bed. He buried his face in the crook of Kye's neck. Kye felt him take a ragged breath. Then he felt the moisture on his neck and realized Sonny was crying. Kye loved his big softy.

He stroked Sonny's back. "I love you. Why are you crying, baby?"

Sonny took another ragged breath. "I can't stop thinking about what would've happened if I hadn't found you last night. You likely would've died alone in that house with me none the wiser. How could you do that to me? How could you just disappear from my life like I don't mean anything?"

Kye's throat swelled. Tears filled his eyes. "I'm so sorry, baby. I don't know why I'm like this. But I swear I'll work on it. I promise I won't run away again. If you hurt my feelings, I'll fight you."

A soft chuckle vibrated against his neck. "Maybe don't start physically fighting me. There's no way I could ever hit you back and no one would believe you're beating me."

Kye hated the idea of anyone hitting Sonny, even him. His hold tightened on Sonny. "If anyone laid a finger on you, I'd scratch their eyes out. You're mine."

"I love you."

The whispered words against Kye's skin had tears rolling back into Kye's hair. He hadn't thought he would hear them again. "I love you too. I'm so sorry. I swear I never meant to break us by buying that house." The tears came harder as the truth hit. Kye had been punishing himself by leaving Sonny. He had been angry with himself. "I genuinely only wanted to get started on spending the rest of my life with you as fast as possible."

Sonny leaned away and held Kye's stare. He looked as big of a mess as Kye felt. "No. I meant what I said, I should've been thrilled. You didn't deserve the way I reacted. I swear if you had demanded I live there, I would've gotten over myself, moved in, and found a different way to contribute. In fact, that's exactly what

I plan to do. You'll never find a better husband. That I promise you."

Kye nodded. "I know. You're always saying you're not good enough for me, but that's such bullshit. We obviously need to work on our communication skills, since we're too used to being single, but we're perfect for each other. You're not better than me and I'm not better than you. We're two halves of the same whole. I know you feel that. We're meant to be together. I can't be the only who feels that."

Sonny played with Kye's hair as he stared down at him. "You're not. I know we're meant to be, and I'll never stop stalking you to the ends of the earth. You should know that by now."

Kye drew Sonny down for a sweet kiss before rubbing noses with him. "Now give me that ring and cuddle with me. I feel like total shit."

Sonny sat back on his heels and found the ring box where it had been knocked aside. After slipping the ring on Kye's finger, he got Kye settled and then spooned the hell out of him. Kye couldn't stop smiling the entire time. While it was beyond obvious they could be dumb as hell, Kye knew in his heart they would always find their way back to each other. They loved each other too much for things to ever be any other way.

·♥·♥·♥·♥·♥·

Hours passed with Sonny holding Kye. He made lunch and they took a shower. Then they went right back to bed so Sonny could hold Kye. Sonny wasn't sure he would ever be able to go back to work without panicking. He couldn't let Kye out of his sight. Every time he walked away for five minutes, he panicked. He worried Kye would disappear or worse. Sonny kept seeing Kye collapse over and over again inside his mind. He had never been so scared. If anything happened to Kye, Sonny would have to crawl into the hole with him, because he wouldn't survive it. They couldn't be apart again.

Around five, Kye finally started to show some signs of life again. His voice turned more animated, and his color improved. He didn't look like he might puke any longer. His hand wouldn't stop finding its way between their bodies, cupping Sonny's cock.

"You're determined to tease me, aren't you?"

He felt more than heard Kye laugh. "Except I'm not teasing."

"You're supposed to be resting."

Kye shrugged. "I have nothing against lazy sex. Not to mention, I didn't think I'd ever get to touch you again. I want to touch you."

Sonny couldn't argue with that point, since he couldn't let go of Kye. Kye's phone rang in the living room. Sonny groaned as he rolled from the bed. He raced to grab it and run it back to Kye before it stopped ringing. It was Kye's mom.

Kye groaned as he glanced at the face, but he still answered. "Hello?"

"I have something to say."

Sonny buried his face against Kye's chest to hide his laughter at Ena's curt tone.

"Okay." Kye dragged out the word, sounding like he knew this conversation could go anywhere.

"We really love Sonny."

Sonny's head shot up at Ena's words. She didn't stop there. "He took us to lunch yesterday and really struggled to talk to us in Japanese. We know not just anyone would do that for us. I hope he knows we're really embarrassed by how we behaved at dinner. He is welcome here anytime and we're really proud of you for finding a good man."

Kye looked like he had been hit by a fast-moving truck. "Um. Thank you. I think he's pretty great too. In fact, he asked me to marry him, and I said yes."

"I know and I knew you would," Ena said, sounding smug. "He asked our permission yesterday."

Kye dropped his chin to stare at Sonny. He traced the line of Sonny's jaw. "He's pretty amazing. I'm glad you guys approve."

"We do. I'll let you go. I know Seth depends on you to do everything around there."

Sonny expected Kye to argue or at least admit to having been to the ER. Instead, Kye said his goodbyes and disconnected the call without saying a word about his incident or admitting he wasn't at work. Kye pulled a face when he obviously read Sonny's expression correctly. "There's no sense in worrying her. It won't happen again. But I can't believe you took my parents to lunch and didn't say a word."

Sonny shrugged as he kissed Kye's chest. "We've had other things on our mind." Kye wore nothing but one of Sonny's t-shirts. Sonny pushed it higher as he spoke. "I've been distracted by this beautiful body in my arms."

Kye's eyes flashed with humor. "Or you didn't want me to know."

While slowly dragging Kye's shirt higher and baring more skin, Sonny shook his head. "I knew Ena wouldn't stay quiet for long."

Despite Kye being hard for him, he still kept talking as if Sonny wasn't trying to seduce him. "You're really amazing. Most people would've written them off after the way they acted at dinner. I hope—when I finally meet your mom—we can have one family introduction go smoothly."

Effectively distracted, Sonny laughed and rolled away long enough to grab his phone. Kye had no idea. Sonny's mom had given birth to him when she had only been sixteen. Now, at forty-nine, his mom lived her best life. She had a sixty-year-old sugar daddy and liked to jet-set around the world. The only reason Kye hadn't met her yet was because she was never around.

Sonny cuddled up next to Kye and called his mom on FaceTime.

She answered on the third ring. "There he is. It's my gorgeous son. How are you, baby?"

Sonny smiled at his mom's happy greeting. She always sounded thrilled to hear from him. "I'm great. How are you?"

Her dark hair billowed in the breeze. It was obvious she was on William's boat. "I'm good. William says hi."

Sonny nodded. "Tell him I said hi. There's someone I want you to meet."

Kye looked horrified. They were in bed and had been all day. Sonny knew Kye would have a few choice words for him when he got off the phone, but he couldn't have Kye worrying about this.

"Oooh, do I finally get to meet the sexy Kye?"

Sonny turned his phone sideways and held it out where his mom could see them both. "Yep. This is him."

Kye waved, looking uncomfortable. "Hi, Ms. Allen."

She laughed. It was a musical sound. "It's just Daisy and it's so nice to finally meet you. Wow. Sonny wasn't exaggerating. You are gorgeous."

Kye blushed, which was something he had never seen. "Thank you, so are you."

A bright smile lit Daisy's face. "You're sweet. I can't wait to meet you in person. William's work takes him all over the world, but I definitely want to make time to see my boys."

Sonny saw his chance to brag. "Kye speaks six languages. I think he'd get along great with William."

"That's amazing."

The praise barely left Daisy's lips before Kye jumped in. "Sonny has learned Japanese."

"That's impressive. You two are too cute."

"We're getting married," Sonny said, incapable of holding back the news any longer.

Daisy pressed her hand to her chest. "That makes me really happy, baby. I can hear the love in your voices. Let me know when and I'll be there. I wouldn't miss it."

"I miss you." The admission was out there before he could stop it. Sonny had a great mom. She had sacrificed a lot over the years for him and he was glad she enjoyed the single life now, but he missed her.

Kye snuggled closer.

Daisy blew him a kiss. "I miss you too, baby. We'll see each other soon. I love you."

"I love you too."

After a few more promises to get together, Sonny disconnected the call. Kye held him.

"That went well," Kye said after a minute passed.

Sonny nodded.

"I like her. She seems great."

Sonny nodded again.

Kye shifted positions and straddled Sonny's hips. "Okay. Seduction time."

A smile exploded across Sonny's face and happiness filled his chest. He was completely in love with the best person he had ever met. Sonny didn't doubt for a second that they would have their ups and downs, but he also knew they would make it. A love like theirs didn't come along every day. Sonny would never take it for granted.

Chapter Eight

♥

SONNY WORKED HIS ROUTE with a huge smile stretching his lips. Nothing got him down anymore since Kye agreed to marry him. Of course, he also had an easy job. It was a lot of heavy lifting, but he met a ton of awesome people. Sonny worked the rich side of town. He got into a lot of penthouses and mansions that most people never saw. For the most part, he dealt with personal assistants and other gatekeepers. Occasionally, he caught glimpses of huge celebrities. It wasn't a bad gig. He didn't have to deal with bosses breathing down his neck and he wasn't stuck at a desk all day.

As he rode the elevator up to the penthouse of the Grand Pointe Hotel, Sonny mentally mused about life. Before meeting Kye, he hadn't realized how truly blessed he was. Nowadays, he saw things a lot clearer.

He was a damn lucky guy. Sonny liked his job, had a great mom, and a wonderful fiancé. He was happy as fuck.

The elevator door opened, and sunlight streamed in, hitting Sonny in the face. Sonny stepped from the elevator and a tiny girl ran inside with a heavily tattooed man hot on her heels. The guy wasn't going to make it before the door closed. Sonny shoved his foot in the door before the elevator could leave with someone's toddler along for the ride.

The guy flashed Sonny a smile as he plucked the girl from the elevator. "Thanks, man. I owe you. She's a fast one and an escape artist." The little girl giggled. Another one around four years old peeked her head around the corner and smiled. Sonny waved at her.

"Is that package for me?"

Sonny remembered why he was there and blushed at his stupidity. "Um. Yeah. Sorry." He met the guy's stare and froze. "Holy... you're Jamie Roussel."

Jamie smiled. "Yep. Is that my package?"

Sonny flipped the box over and checked the name. "Yep. Jamie Roussel." He handed the box to Jamie. "My fiancé will die. You're his all-time favorite singer."

Jamie motioned with the package for Sonny to follow him and spoke over his shoulder as he went. "What's your fiancé's name?"

"Kye."

Jamie set his daughter on the floor next to the coffee table. "You can tell Kye you saved my life with this package." He opened the box. Coloring books and crayons spilled onto the table as he dumped out the contents. Both girls squealed in delight and dove in.

A blindingly beautiful man strolled into the room. "Did the girls get their art supplies? Thank god."

Jamie motioned the man's way. "This is my husband, Hawke. Hawke, this is..."

"Sonny," Sonny supplied.

Jamie nodded. "Sonny. He just rescued Kera from the elevator."

Hawke's shoulders fell. "Again?"

Jamie flashed Sonny a tired look. "Our youngest is Houdini. It's exhausting."

Hawke nodded. "Thank you for catching her. I'll be glad when we're back home. Our house is escape artist proof. This penthouse is too high up with too many exits. I haven't slept in a week."

Sonny smiled. "It's no problem."

Jamie slapped Sonny's back. "Sonny says I'm his fiancé's favorite." He made the claim, sounding exactly like a kid telling everyone he was his mom's favorite.

A bright smile lit Hawke's face. It was obvious he was accustomed to Jamie acting like a kid and he loved it. "Is that so?" Hawke focused on Sonny. "When are you two getting married?"

Sonny beamed at the question. "Tomorrow, actually."

"Perfect. We'll be there," Jamie said, shocking the hell out of Sonny.

"Seriously?"

Jamie nodded. "Sure. You saved my girl, and I can't miss my biggest fan's wedding. Spill the deets so we can plot how to wow your man."

Even though Sonny couldn't believe Jamie fucking Roussel would actually show up to his wedding, he didn't hesitate to fill in the details. If nothing else, he had one hell of a story to tell Kye later. For the millionth time, reality hit like a ton of bricks. Come tomorrow, he would be married to his best friend and the love his life. That was even more surreal than an internationally famous singer and song writer making plans to come to his wedding. He was pretty sure nothing could top loving Kye.

Despite his bad nerves and last-minute minor disasters —like the cake turning out wrong—Kye was happy as fuck. In minutes, he would walk down the aisle with Sonny. They would exchange their vows and spend the rest of their lives together. There was nothing that could top that or make him happier.

They had decided they would walk down the aisle as a couple. As the music began, Kye looked Sonny's way. He looked sexy as sin in his tux. Kye couldn't wait to strip him.

Sonny winked. "Are you ready?"

"We should run," Kye said, feeling spontaneous.

A smile exploded across Sonny's face. "Let's do it."

As one, they sprinted down the aisle, laughing like idiots. Kye didn't care what anyone thought. They were happy and they had done a lot of stupid shit, nearly ruining their shot at love. Now Kye couldn't marry Sonny fast enough. As they came to skidding stop at the altar, Kye caught sight of the laughing face waiting for them.

"Holy shit. You're Jamie Roussel."

Everyone behind them laughed.

All Kye could do was blink. "What the fuck?" Sonny chuckled and it hit Kye. He had done this. Kye looked his way. He didn't know how, but Sonny had turned this wedding into the perfect fan experience for Kye. "What the fuck?"

Sonny swiped at his eyes, laughing. "I told him you'd react this way."

"You know Jamie Roussel?" The shock wouldn't ebb.

"He saved my daughter," Jamie said, answering for Sonny.

Kye couldn't stop looking between them. "You saved Jamie Roussel's daughter." He didn't know why he couldn't wrap his head around anything.

"While you're in the mood for questions, do you take this man to be your lawfully wedded husband?"

Kye looked Jamie's way. "Of course."

Jamie looked at Sonny. "Do you?"

"I do."

Jamie beamed. "Well, then by the power vested in me by the great internets, I pronounce you happy husbands. May you have even half the happiness I have with my better half. Please kiss. I like to watch."

Kye still hadn't recovered from the shock before he found himself in Sonny's arms. People cheered and Kye lost himself in Sonny's kiss. Damn. They were really married. It was the best day of his life.

Kye didn't recover from his surprise until halfway through the first dance. "Holy shit. Jamie and Hawke

Roussel are really at our wedding. And you say you don't contribute to our relationship."

Sonny shook with laughter. The sound vibrated against Kye's ear, making him sigh. "It was a complete fluke. In fact, I still had another ordained person on standby in case Jamie was only fucking with me when he offered to marry us."

"Wow." Even Kye heard the wonder in his voice.

"I know," Sonny said, sounding equally blown away. "I honestly didn't think he was serious when he said he could be here."

Kye shook his head. "No. Not that. I can't believe you married me. I feel like the luckiest man in the world. You're really my husband. That's... wow."

Kye honestly never dreamed there was this much happiness in the entire world. Sonny danced Kye into an empty room off the ballroom inside Seth's home. The moment they were alone, Sonny backed Kye against the wall behind the door, where no one could find them. Their mouths clashed. He could still hear the music playing and Jamie being the life of the party. Kye knew he should care he was having the wedding of a lifetime, just out of sight. Nothing mattered to him except Sonny's hands on his body and the happiness bursting inside him.

"There you two are," Jamie said, popping into view from nowhere. He snagged Kye's hand, pulling him away from Sonny. "It's my turn to dance with your man."

Kye almost said no, but Sonny looked too proud of his surprise wedding gift that Kye couldn't deny him this moment. He went willingly and enjoyed the world's best reception. Kye did it with a smile because he knew he would get to spend the rest of his life living happily ever after with the man of his dreams. Nothing could top that.

Please consider leaving a review at the retailer where you purchased this book. Reviews really help with a book's visibility, which allows me to continue writing more stories. Thank you, Charity.

About the Author

♥

Charity Parkerson is an award-winning and multi-published author with several companies. Born with no filter from her brain to her mouth, she decided to take this odd quirk and insert it in her characters.

*Eight-time Readers' Favorite Award Winner

*2015 Passionate Plume Award Finalist

*2013 Reviewers' Choice Award Winner

*2012 ARRA Finalist for Favorite Paranormal Romance

*Five-time winner of The Mistress of the Darkpath

Connect with her online:

—Sign up for my newsletter: https://sendfox.com/charityparkerson

—Join my readers' group on Facebook: http://bit.ly/CharitysTribe

—Website: charityparkerson.com

—Facebook: facebook.com/authorCharityParkersonfacebook.com/TheMenofSin—Twitter: twitter.com/CharityParkerso

—Instagram: Instagram.com/sinnerauthor

—Bookbub: https://www.bookbub.com/authors/charity-parkerson

—Amazon page: author.to/

—TikTok:

http://www.tiktok.com/@charityparkerson